Candy Cane Lane

THE SWEET SEASONS COLLECTION

KAYLA LOWE

Want a free book? Sign up to my newsletter to get my award-winning book for free! www.authorkaylalowe.com

More of My Books

<u>Series</u>

<u>Christmas Blessings</u>

<u>Christmas Miracle for Two</u>
<u>A Christmas Promise of Love</u>
<u>A Christmas of Renewed Faith</u>

<u>Women of the Bible Fiction</u>

<u>Ruth</u>
<u>Esther</u>
<u>Rachel</u>
<u>Hannah</u>
<u>Deborah</u>

<u>Charms of the Chaste Court</u>

A Courtship in Covent Garden
Whispers in Westminster
Romance in Regent's Park
Serenade on Strand Street
Treasure in Tower Bridge

<u>Sweet Honey by the Sea</u>

<u>The Beekeeper's Secret (Book 1)</u>
<u>A Royal Honeycomb (Book 2)</u>
<u>Bees in Blossom (Book 3)</u>
<u>Honeyed Kisses (Book 4)</u>
<u>Blooming Forever (Book 5)</u>

<u>Strawberry Beach Series</u>

<u>Beachside Lessons (Book 1)</u>
<u>Beachside Lessons (Book 2)</u>
<u>Beachside Lessons (Book 3)</u>

Panama City Beach Series

Sun-Kissed Secrets (Book 1)
Sun-Kissed Secrets (Book 2)
Sun-Kissed Secrets (Book 3)

The Tainted Love Saga

Of Love and Deception (Book 1)
Of Love and Family (Book 2)
Of Love and Violence (Book 3)

Of Love and Abuse(Book 4)
Of Love and Crime (Book 5)
Of Love and Addiction (Book 6)
Of Love and Redemption (Book 7)

Standalones

Maiden's Blush

Poetry

Phantom Poetry
Lost and Found

Chapter One

Frankie Laurie's Mini Cooper sputtered to a stop at the edge of Candy Cane Lane, its engine protesting the long journey. She peered through the windshield, her green eyes widening at the sight before her. Candy Cane Lane stretched out like a ribbon of Christmas cheer, each house more festive than the last.

"Oh my jingle bells," Frankie whispered, her breath fogging the glass. "This is even better than I imagined!"

She hopped out of the car, her curls bouncing as she twirled to take in the full view. The scent of pine and cinnamon wafted through the crisp air, and she could almost taste the promise of hot cocoa on her tongue.

Frankie grabbed her well-worn suitcase, plastered with stickers from past events, and made her way to the Candy Cane Lane Inn. The old building stood proudly at the end of the lane, its gingerbread trim and twinkling lights a warm welcome.

As she pushed open the heavy wooden door, a wave of warmth enveloped her. The lobby was a cozy haven of overstuffed chairs and crackling fireplaces.

"Well, bless my soul! You must be Frankie," a cheerful voice called out. An older woman with silver hair and rosy cheeks bustled over. "I'm Martha, the innkeeper. Welcome to Candy Cane Lane!"

Frankie's face lit up with a megawatt smile. "It's wonderful to meet you, Martha! This place is like stepping into a Christmas card."

Martha chuckled, her eyes twinkling. "Oh honey, you ain't seen nothing yet. Candy Cane Lane's been celebrating Christmas in style since 1892."

As Martha checked her in, Frankie's mind whirled with possibilities for the festival. "I'd love to hear more about the town's history," she said eagerly. "It might spark some ideas for the event."

"Well, pull up a chair by the fire, and I'll tell you all about it," Martha offered, gesturing to a cozy nook. "It all started with old Ebenezer Springsteen..."

Frankie settled in, her notebook at the ready,

feeling for all the world like she'd found a home away from home. As Martha's tales unfolded, Frankie's heart swelled with excitement. This wasn't just a job; it was a chance to be part of something truly special.

As Martha wove tales of Christmases past, Frankie found herself drifting back to the moment she first learned about Candy Cane Lane. She had been sitting in her cramped city office, surrounded by the chaos of half-finished event plans and the constant hum of traffic outside, when an email from the town council caught her eye.

"Seeking event planner to revive annual Christmas festival," the subject line read. Intrigued, Frankie opened the message and was immediately captivated by the attached photos of Candy Cane Lane in all its holiday glory. The colorful houses, the glowing lights, and the sense of community that seemed to radiate from every image struck a chord deep within her.

As she read on, learning about the town's rich history and the importance of the festival, Frankie felt a growing sense of excitement. This was more than just another event. It was a chance to be part of something truly meaningful. She could already picture the joy on children's faces as they sipped hot cocoa and listened to carolers, the laughter of families as they strolled down the lane admiring the decorations.

In that moment, Frankie knew she had to be a part of this. She had been feeling restless in the city, longing for a change of pace and a chance to make a real difference. Candy Cane Lane seemed like the perfect opportunity to do just that.

She responded to the email immediately, pouring her heart into her proposal. She shared her vision for the festival, her ideas for new traditions and activities that would bring the community together like never before. When the town council called to offer her the job, Frankie couldn't contain her excitement.

Now, sitting in the cozy inn and listening to Martha's stories, Frankie felt a sense of belonging wash over her. The warmth of the fireplace seemed to seep into her bones, chasing away the chill of the city and filling her with a renewed sense of purpose.

As Martha finished her tale, Frankie leaned forward, her eyes sparkling with determination. "Martha, I promise you this will be the best Christmas festival Candy Cane Lane has ever seen," she declared, her voice filled with conviction. "I'm going to pour my heart and soul into making it unforgettable."

Martha smiled, reaching out to pat Frankie's

hand. "I have no doubt about that, dear. There's something special about you, and I think this town is lucky to have you here."

With those words ringing in her ears, Frankie settled back into her chair, her mind already whirling with ideas. She could hardly wait to get started, to bring her vision to life and create a Christmas celebration that would be remembered for generations to come. Here in Candy Cane Lane, surrounded by the magic of the season, anything seemed possible.

Chapter Two

The sawdust-filled workshop echoed with the rhythmic sound of sandpaper against wood as Sean Morrison carefully smoothed the edges of a custom-made bookshelf. His brow furrowed in concentration, strong hands moving with practiced precision. A glance at the clock made him sigh.

"Grace, sweetheart!" he called out. "Time to pack up your homework. We need to head to the hardware store before it closes."

A patter of small feet approached, and Sean's eight-year-old daughter appeared in the doorway, her dark hair in messy pigtails. "But Dad, I'm not finished with my math yet."

Sean set down his tools and knelt to her level, his

brown eyes softening. "I know, pumpkin. We'll finish it together after dinner, okay? Right now, I need to pick up supplies for Mrs. Johnson's rocking chair."

As they drove through town, Sean's mind raced with his ever-growing to-do list. The holidays always brought an influx of orders, and while he was grateful for the work, balancing it with single parenthood was a constant juggling act.

The bell above the hardware store door chimed as they entered. Sean nodded a quiet greeting to Tom, the owner, before heading to the wood stains aisle. He was examining different shades when a flash of auburn curls caught his eye.

A petite woman with vibrant green eyes was struggling to reach a high shelf, determination etched on her face. Without thinking, Sean stepped forward.

"Excuse me, ma'am. Can I help you with that?" he offered, his voice low and hesitant.

The woman turned, her face lighting up with a brilliant smile that caught Sean off guard. "Oh, that would be wonderful! I'm trying to get that string of fairy lights up there."

As Sean easily retrieved the item, the woman continued, her words tumbling out in a rush of enthusiasm. "I'm Frankie, by the way. Frankie Laurie.

I'm here to plan the Christmas festival, and I had this vision of twinkling lights cascading from the town square gazebo like a waterfall of stars. Do you think that's too much? Sometimes I get carried away with the magic of it all."

Sean blinked, momentarily overwhelmed by her energy. "Uh, no, that sounds...nice," he managed, handing her the lights. "I'm Sean. Sean Morrison."

Frankie's eyes widened in recognition. "Oh! You must be the carpenter everyone's been raving about. Your work is supposed to be amazing."

Sean felt heat creep up his neck, uncomfortable with the praise. "I do alright," he mumbled, taking a step back. "Good luck with your festival plans."

As he turned to go, Frankie called out, "Wait! I'd love to hear your thoughts on some of my ideas. Maybe over coffee sometime?"

Sean hesitated, an inexplicable mix of panic and intrigue rising in his chest. "I...I'm pretty busy these days. But thanks," he replied, his tone more brusque than he intended.

As he hurried back to Grace, Sean couldn't shake the feeling that he'd just missed out on something. But the thought of even having coffee with another woman still felt like a betrayal to his late wife's memory. With a deep breath, he pushed the interaction from his mind, focusing instead on the warmth of his daughter's small hand in his as they finished their errands.

The bell above the hardware store door chimed as Sean and Grace stepped out into the crisp winter air again the next day. This time of year, it seemed trips to the hardware store were a daily occurrence.

Grace's eyes lit up as she spotted Frankie arranging a display of festive ornaments on a nearby storefront.

"Dad, look! It's the Christmas lady!" Grace exclaimed, tugging on Sean's hand. Before he could protest, his daughter was pulling him towards Frankie with surprising strength for her small frame.

Frankie turned, her face breaking into a warm smile as she saw them approach. "Well, hello there!" she greeted, kneeling down to Grace's level. "I'm Frankie. What's your name, sweetheart?"

"I'm Grace," the little girl replied, her shyness melting away in the face of Frankie's infectious enthusiasm. "Are you making everything Christmassy?"

Frankie nodded, her green eyes twinkling.

"That's right! I'm here to help make this the most magical Christmas Candy Cane Lane has ever seen. Do you like Christmas, Grace?"

Grace's face lit up like a string of fairy lights. "I love Christmas! It's my favorite holiday ever!"

Sean watched in amazement as Grace and Frankie launched into an animated discussion about their favorite Christmas traditions, decorations, and treats. His daughter, usually reserved around strangers, was chattering away as if she'd known Frankie for years.

"And what about you, Sean?" Frankie asked, glancing up at him. "What's your favorite part of Christmas?"

Sean hesitated, caught off guard by the question. "I, uh...I guess I like the quiet moments," he admitted softly. "Like when the house is all decorated, and it's just peaceful."

Frankie's smile softened, a flicker of understanding passing between them. "Those are beautiful moments," she agreed. Then, turning back to Grace, she asked, "Would you like to help me hang some ornaments, sweetie?"

As Grace eagerly assisted Frankie, Sean found himself drawn into their cheerful conversation. The weight on his shoulders seemed to lighten just a bit as he watched his daughter laugh and play, her joy as bright as the twinkling lights around them.

Later, as they strolled down Candy Cane Lane, Frankie's curiosity got the better of her. "So, tell me about this street," she prompted. "I've never seen a place quite like it."

Sean's expression grew contemplative. "Candy Cane Lane has been a Candy Cane Lane tradition for generations," he explained. "Every year, the whole community comes together to decorate it." He motioned to the candy cane-lined streets. "I guess you can see where the town gets its name."

Frankie listened intently, her heart swelling with the beauty of it all. "That's incredible," she breathed. "But why is this year so special?"

Sean's eyes grew distant. "This is the 50th anniversary of Candy Cane Lane," he said softly. "And...it might be the last. The town's been struggling lately. Some folks think it's time to let the tradition go."

Frankie's determination sparked in her eyes. "Well, we can't let that happen," she declared. "This festival is going to remind everyone why Candy Cane Lane matters. It's going to bring back the magic."

As they walked back down Candy Cane Lane towards the inn, Sean found himself sneaking glances at Frankie. The way her auburn curls bounced with each step, the sparkle in her green eyes as she took in the festive decorations, the genuine warmth in her smile...He couldn't help but be drawn to her vibrant energy. It was like she radiated Christmas cheer with every breath.

And then there was the way Grace had taken to her so quickly. His daughter was usually shy around new people, but with Frankie, she had opened up immediately, chattering away about her favorite Christmas ornaments and holiday treats. Seeing the two of them together, heads bent over a box of delicate glass baubles, something stirred in Sean's chest.

It had been so long since Grace had a maternal figure in her life. Not since...He swallowed hard, pushing away the painful memories that threatened to surface. But watching Frankie with Grace, so natural and loving, Sean couldn't help but wonder if maybe, just maybe, this was exactly what they both needed.

As they reached the inn's front steps, Frankie turned to him, her cheeks flushed from the cold land her eyes aglow. "Thank you for walking us back, Sean. And for sharing those stories about Candy Cane Lane. I feel like I understand this place so much better now."

Sean ducked his head, unused to such direct appreciation. "It was nothing," he mumbled, scuffing his boot on the bottom step.

But Frankie laid a gentle hand on his arm, and he glanced up to meet her earnest gaze. "It wasn't nothing," she insisted softly. "It meant a lot to me. And I think it meant a lot to Grace too."

At the mention of his daughter, Sean's heart clenched. He looked over to where Grace was admiring the inn's gingerbread trim, her little face alight with wonder. When was the last time he'd seen her so carefree? So...happy?

A sudden realization hit him like a snowball to the face. Frankie's arrival in Springbrook, her determination to save the Christmas festival and bring back the magic of Candy Cane Lane—it wasn't just about the town. It was about healing. The community, Grace...and maybe even himself.

He turned back to Frankie, seeing her in a new light. He'd barely met her, but in the short time he'd known her, he could already tell she poured her whole heart into everything she did. She found joy in the smallest details and shared that joy so freely with others... It was more than just Christmas spirit. It was a rare and precious gift.

Swallowing hard, Sean managed a small smile.

"Thank you, Frankie. For everything you're doing for Candy Cane Lane. I didn't realize how much this town needed someone like you until..."

He trailed off, suddenly self-conscious. But Frankie seemed to understand. Her hand squeezed his arm gently before falling away.

"Until now," she finished for him, her voice soft with understanding. "Sometimes it takes an outsider's perspective to remind us of the magic that's been right in front of us all along."

Sean nodded, his throat tight. "Yeah. I guess you're right."

Frankie's smile turned playful. "I usually am," she teased, then sobered. "But really, I'm just honored to be a part of this community, even for a little while. And I'm grateful to have met you and Grace."

Sean found himself returning her smile, a real one this time. "The feeling is mutual."

As Frankie bid them goodnight and disappeared into the warmth of the inn with a parting wave, Sean felt a flicker of something he hadn't experienced in a long time—hope. Hope for the festival, for the town...and maybe even for his own heart.

He reached for Grace's hand, marveling at how small it still was in his own. "What do you say we head home, Gracie-girl? I think we've had enough excitement for one day."

Grace nodded, stifling a yawn. But as they walked back to the truck, she tugged on his hand. "Dad? I like Miss Frankie. She makes Christmas feel extra special."

Sean's heart stumbled in his chest. "Yeah, sweetheart. She sure does."

That night, as Sean tucked Grace into bed, his mind kept drifting back to Frankie. Her passion for the festival, her easy way with Grace, the sparkle in her eyes that rivaled the lights of Candy Cane Lane...He couldn't seem to shake her from his thoughts.

He wandered into the living room, his gaze falling on the framed photo of his late wife that sat on the mantel. Guilt twisted in his gut as he picked it up, tracing the familiar lines of her face with his finger.

"Am I betraying your memory?" he whispered to the silent room. "By even considering..." He couldn't finish the thought.

But as he stared into the eyes of the woman he'd loved and lost, he could almost hear her gentle voice in his ear. *It's okay, Sean. It's time. You deserve to be happy again.*

A single tear tracked down his cheek as he set the photo back in its place. Maybe, just maybe, it was time to open his heart to the possibility of love once more. And maybe, in the magic of Candy Cane Lane at Christmastime, he'd find the courage to take that chance.

Chapter Three

The next morning dawned bright and cold, the air crisp with the promise of snow. Frankie was up with the sun, her mind already buzzing with ideas for the festival. She had a meeting with the town council today to pitch her vision, and she wanted everything to be perfect.

She spent the morning transforming the inn's cozy meeting room into a winter wonderland, hanging twinkling lights and draping garlands of evergreen along the walls. She set up a small Christmas tree in the corner, adorning it with handmade ornaments that showcased the charm and history of Springbrook. On the table, she arranged a tray of festive treats—gingerbread cookies, peppermint bark, and steaming mugs of hot cocoa topped with fluffy marshmallows.

As the council members began to arrive, Frankie greeted each one with a warm smile and a candy cane. But her nerves fluttered when an old lady who pronounced herself "Edith Morrison" walked in, her sharp eyes taking in the decorations with a skeptical frown.

"Quite the setup you've got here, young lady," Edith remarked, her tone more critical than complimentary. "I hope you're not planning on making too many changes to our traditions."

Frankie took a deep breath, reminding herself to stay positive. "Of course not, Mrs. Morrison. I only want to enhance the festival, to remind everyone of the magic that's always been here in Candy Cane Lane."

After all the member filed in and got situated, Frankie stood before the town committee, her heart racing with excitement and nerves. The small room felt cozy, with its wood-paneled walls adorned with vintage Christmas decorations. The scent of cinnamon and pine wafted through the air, a reminder of the season's spirit.

"Ladies and gentlemen," Frankie began, her voice warm and enthusiastic, "I present to you 'Candy

Cane Lane: A Golden Christmas Journey.'" She gestured to the mood board she'd prepared, filled with twinkling lights, golden accents, and nostalgic touches.

As she explained her vision, Frankie noticed a few committee members leaning forward, interest sparkling in their eyes. However, she couldn't help but notice the frown deepening on the face of Edith seated near the end of the table.

"We'll transform Candy Cane Lane into a living timeline," Frankie continued, her hands moving animatedly. "Each house will represent a decade from the past fifty years, showcasing how Christmas traditions have evolved while staying true to Candy Cane Lane's heart."

"That sounds lovely, dear," Sean's aunt interjected, her voice laced with skepticism. "But we've always done things a certain way here. Why fix what isn't broken?"

Frankie took a deep breath, reminding herself to stay positive. "I completely understand your perspective, ma'am. Traditions are precious. But imagine blending the old with the new, creating something that honors the past while exciting the next generation. Plus, respectfully, the town did reach out for help. I know you need to boost tourism to stay afloat, and I am very well experienced with doing that. I have an extensive marketing reach that I believe will truly put your charming little town on the map this Christmas and see your profits soaring."

A murmur rippled through the room, but Frankie continued on.

"Change can be scary," Frankie acknowledged, her voice softening. "But sometimes, it's exactly what we need to remind us why we fell in love with something in the first place. Let's make this anniversary unforgettable, a celebration that will ensure Candy Cane Lane's legacy for another fifty years."

As Frankie finished her pitch, she held her breath, hoping her words had touched their hearts as deeply as Candy Cane Lane had touched hers.

Chapter Four

Snowflakes danced through the air as Frankie bustled across the town square, her arms laden with garlands and twinkling lights. Despite the chill, her cheeks were rosy with excitement. This year's Christmas festival would be the most magical one yet, if she had anything to say about it.

Just as she began draping the first strand of lights around a lamppost, a fierce gust of wind nearly knocked her off her feet. Frankie's eyes widened as she took in the darkening sky. The flurries were quickly turning into a full-fledged blizzard.

"Oh no," she muttered, gathering up her supplies. "Not now, not when there's still so much to do!"

Ducking her head against the swirling snow, Frankie made a beeline for the cozy café on the corner. At least she could wait out the worst of the storm with a steaming mug of hot cocoa. As she pushed open the door, the cheerful jingle of bells and the aroma of freshly baked cookies enveloped her.

Frankie's gaze swept the crowded room, searching for an empty seat, when a familiar voice piped up: "Miss Frankie! Over here!"

Little Grace Morrison waved enthusiastically from a table by the window, where she sat across from her father, Sean. Frankie's heart did a little flip as their eyes met. She'd be lying if she said she hadn't been hoping to run into the handsome carpenter again.

With a bright smile, Frankie wove her way through the tables. "Hello there! Fancy meeting you two here on this blustery day."

Sean shifted in his seat, looking slightly uncom-fortable. "Grace, I'm sure Miss Frankie has other things to-"

"She should sit with us. No one should be alone in a snowstorm." Grace declared with all the authority an eight-year-old could muster.

Frankie bit back a grin at the girl's precocious insistence. "Well, if you insist..." She slid into the chair beside Grace, secretly thrilled at the prospect of spending more time with the intriguing father-daughter duo.

As the snow continued to fall in thick, swirling flakes outside, the three of them fell into easy conversation. Grace chattered animatedly about her Christmas wish list, while Sean listened with a fond, if slightly wistful, expression.

Watching them together, Frankie couldn't help but wonder about Sean's story. There was a sadness in his eyes that hinted at a deep loss, yet the love he had for his daughter shone through in every interaction. She found herself wanting to know more, to understand the man behind the guarded exterior.

The café bustled with activity as patrons sought refuge from the unrelenting snowstorm. Frankie cradled her mug of hot cocoa, savoring the warmth that seeped into her hands. She glanced at Sean, who seemed engrossed in his thoughts, his brow furrowed slightly.

"So, Sean," Frankie began, her voice cutting through the comfortable silence, "Grace mentioned you're quite the carpenter. I could really use some help with the festival decorations if you're willing."

Sean's eyes widened in surprise. "Oh, I don't know...I have a lot on my plate already."

"Please, Daddy!" Grace pleaded, her eyes shining with excitement. "It would be so much fun to work on the festival together!"

Sean's resolve wavered under his daughter's hopeful gaze. He sighed, a small smile tugging at the corners of his mouth. "Alright. I suppose we could lend a hand."

Frankie clapped her hands in delight. "Fantastic! I promise it'll be a blast. Plus, it's for a good cause—bringing some holiday cheer to Candy Cane Lane."

As they finished their drinks and bundled up to brave the snowy streets, Frankie couldn't help but feel a flutter of anticipation in her chest. There was something about Sean that intrigued her, a depth and kindness that drew her in.

The snow had finally let up, blanketing the town in a pristine layer of white. Frankie and Sean made their way to the festival site, their breath forming little puffs of steam in the crisp air. Grace skipped ahead, her laughter ringing out like silver bells.

"I really appreciate you helping out," Frankie said, glancing at Sean. "I know it's short notice, but I have a feeling you're going to be a lifesaver."

Sean ducked his head, a hint of a smile playing on his lips. "Happy to lend a hand. Grace is over the moon about it, and well, I couldn't say no to her. Or to you."

Frankie felt a blush creep into her cheeks at his words. There was something about the way he said it, a warmth that made her heart skip a beat.

As they reached the festival grounds, Frankie led them to a half-finished display—a towering Christmas tree that would serve as the centerpiece. Garlands and ornaments were scattered around its base, waiting to be arranged.

"This is where your expertise comes in," Frankie explained, gesturing to the tree. "I have a vision, but I'm afraid my carpentry skills are a bit lacking."

Sean assessed the structure, his brow furrowed in concentration. "I think I can work with this. We'll need to secure the base and add some support beams, but it's doable."

As they set to work, Frankie couldn't help but admire the way Sean's hands moved with such precision and skill. He seemed to come alive when he was creating something, a sense of purpose and passion radiating from him.

Grace flitted between them, eager to help in any way she could. She handed them tools and ornaments, her face alight with joy. Frankie's heart swelled at the sight, marveling at the little girl's resilience and spirit.

Hours passed in a flurry of activity, punctuated by laughter and easy conversation. As the sun began to dip below the horizon, they stepped back to admire their handiwork. The Christmas tree stood tall and proud, its branches adorned with twinkling lights and shimmering ornaments.

"It's perfect," Frankie breathed, her eyes shining with delight. "Sean, you've worked wonders."

Sean rubbed the back of his neck, a shy smile on his face. "It was a team effort. I couldn't have done it without you and Grace."

Grace beamed up at them, her cheeks rosy from the cold. "Daddy, can we come back tomorrow to help Miss Frankie with more decorations? Please?"

Sean hesitated for a moment, and Frankie held her breath, hoping he would say yes. Finally, he nodded, his eyes softening as he looked at his daughter. "Sure, sweetheart. We can come back tomorrow."

As they parted ways, Frankie's heart warmed with something she couldn't quite identify but something that left her smiling.

The next day, despite the lingering snowfall, Frankie and Sean met at the community center to begin work on the Christmas display. The room was filled with the scent of fresh pine and the soft strains of holiday music.

"I have to admit," Frankie said, surveying the array of wooden pieces scattered across the worktable, "I'm not exactly a master carpenter. But I'm a quick learner!"

Sean chuckled, the sound warm and rich. "Don't worry, I'll guide you through it. It's all about patience and attention to detail."

As they worked side by side, measuring and cutting the wood, Frankie found herself drawn to Sean's quiet strength and gentle manner. He took the time to explain each step, his hands deftly demonstrating the techniques.

Hours passed, filled with laughter, conversation, and the satisfying progress of their creation. Frankie marveled at how Sean's guarded exterior seemed to melt away as they worked, revealing glimpses of the caring, compassionate man beneath.

"You know," Frankie said softly, pausing to admire their handiwork, "there's something special about creating something beautiful together. It's like a little bit of magic."

Sean met her gaze, his eyes holding a newfound warmth. "You're right. It's been a long time since I've felt this sense of...purpose. Thank you, Frankie."

Frankie's heart swelled at his words, a blush coloring her cheeks. "I should be thanking you. Your skills are bringing this display to life."

As they stood there, surrounded by the fruits of their labor and the twinkling lights of the Christmas decorations, Frankie couldn't help but feel that this was just the beginning of something truly special—a connection forged through faith, creativity, and the magic of the holiday season.

Grace burst into the workshop, her cheeks rosy from the cold and her eyes sparkling with excitement. "Frankie! Daddy! Look what I made!" She held up a handmade Christmas card, covered in glitter and featuring a clumsily drawn Christmas tree.

Frankie knelt down to admire the card, a warm smile spreading across her face. "Gracie, this is beautiful! You're quite the artist."

The little girl beamed with pride, then turned to Sean, her expression growing serious. "Daddy, can I tell you my Christmas wish?"

Sean's eyes softened as he knelt beside his daughter. "Of course, sweetheart. What is it?"

Grace took a deep breath, her small hands fidgeting with the card. "I wish...I wish for you to be happy again, Daddy. Like you used to be."

Frankie felt her heart constrict at the child's words, a lump forming in her throat. She watched as Sean pulled Grace into a tight hug, his voice thick with emotion. "Oh, Gracie. I am happy, because I have you."

Grace pulled back, her eyes searching her father's face. "But you're not the same, Daddy. Not since Mommy went to heaven."

Sean swallowed hard, his gaze flickering to Frankie for a moment. "I know, baby. It's been hard, but I promise you, I'm trying."

As Frankie witnessed this tender moment between father and daughter, she felt a surge of empathy and a deep longing to help Sean find the happiness Grace wished for him. She knew all too well the transformative power of faith and the magic of Christmas.

When Grace scampered off to play, Frankie turned to Sean, her voice gentle. "You know, Sean, I understand what it's like to feel lost and alone. There was a time in my life when I felt like I had nothing to hold onto."

Sean met her gaze, his eyes reflecting a glimmer of vulnerability. "What changed?"

Frankie smiled softly, her hand instinctively reaching for the small cross pendant she wore. "I found my faith. It was like a beacon of hope in the darkness, guiding me back to the joy and purpose I thought I'd lost."

She took a step closer, her voice filled with conviction. "That's why I love Christmas so much. It's a time when we celebrate the greatest gift of all— the birth of Jesus, the ultimate symbol of hope and love. It's a reminder that we're never truly alone."

Sean listened intently, his expression thoughtful. "I want to believe that, Frankie. I really do. But sometimes, it feels like the weight of the world is on my shoulders, and I don't know how to let it go."

Frankie reached out, her hand resting gently on his arm. "That's where faith comes in, Sean. It's about trusting in something greater than ourselves, knowing that we don't have to carry our burdens alone. And it's about finding joy in the little things, like creating special moments for the people we love."

As they stood there, surrounded by the warmth of the workshop and the glow of the Christmas lights, Frankie could see a flicker of hope in Sean's eyes—a glimmer of the happiness Grace had wished for. And in that moment, she knew that with faith, love, and a little Christmas magic, anything was possible.

Chapter Five

Sean sat in his living room, the warm glow of the fireplace casting dancing shadows on the walls. He cradled a mug of hot cocoa, its sweet aroma mingling with the scent of the pine garland draped across the mantel. Despite the cozy atmosphere, his mind was restless, replaying the day's events and Frankie's heartfelt words.

He couldn't help but smile as he recalled her infectious enthusiasm and the way her eyes sparkled when she spoke about her faith and love for Christmas. It was a kind of joy he hadn't encountered in a long time, and it stirred something deep within him.

As he took a sip of the rich, velvety cocoa, his gaze drifted to the framed photograph on the side table—a picture of his late wife, her radiant smile forever captured in time. A familiar ache bloomed in his chest, a bittersweet mixture of love and loss.

His fingers tracing the edge of the frame. "I wish you were here to see this. To see Grace's excitement and the way the town is coming together. You always loved Christmas so much."

Memories of past holidays flooded his mind— the laughter, the warmth, the love that filled their home. But now, those memories were tinged with sadness, a reminder of what he had lost.

Yet, as he thought of Frankie's words, a flicker of hope ignited in his heart. Perhaps she was right. Maybe it was time to open himself up to the possibility of joy again, to embrace the magic of the season and the love that still surrounded him.

Sean set down his mug and walked over to the window, gazing out at the twinkling lights that adorned the neighborhood. The soft, white glow seemed to beckon him, inviting him to step out of the shadows and into the light.

With a deep breath, he made a decision. He would honor his late wife's memory by living life to the fullest, by cherishing the precious moments with Grace and allowing himself to find happiness once more. It wouldn't be easy, but with faith and the support of those around him, he knew he could take that first step.

As Sean stood at the window, lost in thought, a soft knock at the door pulled him back to the present. He padded across the room, his socked feet sinking into the plush carpet, and opened the door to find Frankie standing on his porch, her cheeks rosy from the cold and a warm smile on her face.

"I hope I'm not interrupting," she said, her breath forming little clouds in the chilly air. "I just wanted to drop off some cookies Grace and I made earlier. She insisted that we save the best ones for her daddy."

Sean's heart swelled with love for his little girl, and he couldn't help but return Frankie's smile. "That's very thoughtful of you both. Please, come in. It's freezing out there."

Frankie stepped inside, the scent of sugar and spice wafting from the basket of cookies she carried. As Sean closed the door behind her, she took in the cozy living room, her eyes sparkling with appreciation. "Your home is lovely, Sean. It feels so warm and inviting."

"Thank you," he replied, gesturing for her to take a seat on the sofa. "I've been trying to make it feel more like Christmas for Grace's sake. She's been through so much."

Frankie nodded, her expression softening with understanding. "You're doing a wonderful job. I can see how much you love and care for her."

As they settled on the sofa, Sean found himself opening up to Frankie in a way he hadn't with anyone in a long time. He spoke of his late wife, the joy she brought to their lives, and the void her absence had left behind. Frankie listened intently, her hand resting gently on his arm in a gesture of comfort and support.

"I can't imagine how difficult it's been for you," she said softly. "But I truly believe that love never dies. Your wife may not be here physically, but her love lives on through you and Grace. And I know she would want you both to find happiness again."

Sean felt a lump form in his throat, moved by Frankie's kind words. "You're right," he said, his voice thick with emotion. "I've been so focused on my own grief that I've forgotten to truly live. But I want to change that, for Grace's sake and for my own."

Frankie smiled, her eyes shining with warmth and understanding. "And you will. One step at a time. And know that you have a whole community here to support you, myself included."

As they continued to talk, the warmth of the fireplace and the sweetness of the cookies creating a cozy atmosphere, Sean felt a glimmer of hope and possibility stirring in his heart. Perhaps, with Frankie's encouragement and the magic of the holiday season, he could learn to embrace joy and love once again.

$$Chapter\ Six$$

Frankie sat cross-legged on the living room floor, surrounded by a colorful array of arts and crafts supplies. Little Grace knelt beside her, tongue poking out in concentration as she carefully glued sequins onto a handmade card.

"Daddy's going to love this," Grace declared, her eyes shining with excitement. "It's gonna be the best surprise ever!"

Frankie grinned, her heart warming at the little girl's enthusiasm. "He sure will, sweetie. You're putting so much love into this card." She reached over to ruffle Grace's curly hair affectionately.

As they worked, Frankie couldn't help but marvel at the bond she'd formed with Grace over the past few days. The girl had doggedly insisted on spending more and more time with her, and who was Frankie to say no to such a precious child? What had started as a business arrangement in Candy Cane Lane had blossomed into something deeper—a genuine connection that filled a space in Frankie's heart she hadn't realized was empty.

The sound of the front door opening drew their attention. "I'm home!" Sean called out, his deep voice echoing through the house.

"Quick, hide everything!" Frankie whispered conspiratorially to Grace, who giggled and scrambled to gather up the supplies.

Sean appeared in the doorway, his eyebrows raised at the flurry of activity. "What are you two up to?"

"It's a secret!" Grace declared, clutching the unfinished card to her chest.

Sean chuckled, holding up his hands in mock surrender. "Alright, alright. I won't pry." His gaze met Frankie's, and a flicker of warmth passed between them.

Grace scampered off to her room to stash the surprise, leaving Sean and Frankie alone. An easy silence settled over them as Frankie began tidying up the remaining craft supplies.

"Thanks for spending time with her," Sean said softly, his eyes full of gratitude. "It means a lot."

Frankie smiled, shaking her head. "It's my pleasure, Sean. Grace is an amazing kid." She hesitated for a moment before adding gently, "I know it hasn't been easy...since you lost your wife. But you're doing an incredible job with her."

Sean's shoulders sagged slightly, a shadow passing over his face. He sank down onto the couch, rubbing a hand over his beard. "Some days are harder than others," he admitted, his voice rough with emotion. "I miss her so much. We both do."

Frankie settled beside him, close enough to offer comfort but not presuming too much. "Grief is a journey," she said softly, reaching out to place a hand on his arm. "It's okay to feel lost sometimes. But I truly believe God has a plan, even when we can't see it."

Sean met her gaze, his brown eyes shining with unshed tears. "I want to believe that. I do. It's just...hard to have faith when it feels like my whole world has been shattered."

"I know," Frankie murmured, giving his arm a gentle squeeze. "But that's the beautiful thing about faith—it's there to guide us through the darkest times. To remind us that we're never alone, even when it feels like it."

A ghost of a smile touched Sean's lips. "You have a way of making things seem a little brighter, Frankie Laurie."

Frankie ducked her head, a blush rising to her cheeks. "Well, I figure the world can always use a bit more light. Especially around the holidays."

Sean nodded, some of the tension easing from his shoulders. "Thank you," he said sincerely, covering her hand with his own. "For everything."

As they sat there, hands clasped and hearts full, Frankie couldn't help but feel that this was exactly where she was meant to be—bringing joy and healing to a family who needed it most.

***

The cheerful jingle of bells filled the air as Frankie rummaged through a box of Christmas decorations, her auburn curls bouncing with each movement. "Aha!" she exclaimed, holding up a glittering star ornament. "This will be perfect for the top of the tree."

Sean glanced up from where he was untangling a string of lights, a bemused expression on his face. "I still can't believe you talked me into this," he said, shaking his head. "Creating a giant Christmas tree for the festival? It's a bit ambitious, don't you think?"

Frankie grinned, her green eyes sparkling with mischief. "Go big or go home, that's my motto," she quipped, carefully placing the star back in the box. "Besides, Candy Cane Lane deserves a centerpiece that will really wow the crowd."

As they worked side by side, Frankie couldn't help but notice the way Sean's hands moved with practiced precision, his strong fingers deftly weaving the lights through the branches. There was a quiet intensity to his focus, a dedication to craftsmanship that she found incredibly attractive.

"You're really good at this," she remarked, gesturing to the tree. "I guess all that woodworking experience comes in handy for more than just furniture-making."

Sean ducked his head, a hint of a smile playing at the corners of his mouth. "Well, I've always enjoyed working with my hands," he admitted. "There's something satisfying about taking raw materials and turning them into something beautiful."

Frankie nodded, understanding the sentiment all too well. "It's like event planning, in a way," she mused. "Taking a blank space and transforming it into something magical, something that brings people together."

As they continued to decorate the tree, their conversation flowed easily, punctuated by laughter and the occasional teasing remark. Frankie found herself drawn to Sean's quiet strength, the way he listened intently and offered insight without judgment.

Before long, the enormous tree was a vision of holiday splendor, its branches dripping with shimmering ornaments and twinkling lights. Frankie stepped back to admire their handiwork, a sense of pride swelling in her chest.

"It's beautiful," she breathed, turning to Sean with a smile. "Thank you for helping me bring this vision to life."

Sean returned her smile, his brown eyes warm and sincere. "I have to admit, your enthusiasm is contagious," he chuckled. "I haven't felt this excited about Christmas in a long time."

As they basked in the glow of the tree, Frankie couldn't help but feel a flicker of hope in her heart. Maybe, just maybe, she was making a difference in Sean's life—and in the lives of everyone in Candy Cane Lane.

The town committee meeting was in full swing, with voices rising and falling as members debated the merits of Frankie's festival ideas. Some were enthusiastic, eager to embrace the change and excitement she brought to the table. Others, however, remained skeptical, clinging to tradition and resistant to anything too unconventional.

Frankie sat at the head of the table, her hands clasped tightly in her lap as she listened to the arguments swirling around her. She knew that change could be difficult, especially for a close-knit community like Candy Cane Lane. But she also knew, with every fiber of her being, that this festival had the power to bring joy and healing to a town that desperately needed it.

As the debate grew more heated, Sean leaned forward in his seat, his brow furrowed with determination. "I think we need to give Frankie's ideas a chance," he said firmly, his voice cutting through the chatter. "She's brought a fresh perspective to this festival, and I believe her vision has the potential to bring our community together in a way we haven't seen in years."

A hush fell over the room as all eyes turned to Sean. Frankie felt a surge of gratitude and affection for the man beside her, amazed by his unwavering support.

"Sean's right," one of the committee members piped up, breaking the silence. "Frankie's ideas may be unconventional, but that's exactly what we need right now. Something to shake things up and remind us all of the magic of the season."

Murmurs of agreement rippled through the room, and Frankie felt a weight lift from her shoulders. She caught Sean's eye, mouthing a silent "thank you" as he smiled back at her.

As the meeting drew to a close, with the majority of the committee now in favor of Frankie's plans, she couldn't help but feel a sense of excitement and purpose.

As the committee members filed out of the room, Frankie turned to Sean, her eyes sparkling with excitement. "I can't thank you enough for standing up for me like that," she said, her voice warm with gratitude. "It means the world to have your support."

Sean ducked his head, a gentle smile playing at the corners of his mouth. "I meant every word," he replied, meeting her gaze. "You've brought something special to this town, Frankie. Something we all needed, even if we didn't know it."

Frankie felt a blush creep into her cheeks at his words, her heart fluttering in her chest. "Speaking of bringing something special," she said, eager to change the subject before her emotions got the better of her, "I was thinking we could start decorating the big tree on Candy Cane Lane this afternoon. What do you say?"

Sean's smile widened, his eyes crinkling at the corners. "I think that's a great idea," he agreed, reaching out to squeeze her hand briefly. "Let me just call Grace's babysitter and let her know I'll be a little late picking her up."

An hour later, Frankie and Sean stood before the towering evergreen, its branches stretching toward the sky like eager arms waiting to be adorned. Boxes of ornaments and strings of twinkling lights lay scattered at their feet, a kaleidoscope of color against the snowy ground.

"Where should we start?" Sean asked, rubbing his hands together in anticipation.

Frankie tapped her chin thoughtfully, surveying the tree with a critical eye. "I think we should start with the lights," she decided, reaching for a tangled strand of glittering bulbs. "They'll create a nice base for the ornaments and really make the tree shine."

Together, they set to work, carefully winding the lights around the tree's branches, their laughter and easy banter filling the crisp winter air. As they worked, Frankie couldn't help but steal glances at Sean, marveling at the way the afternoon sun played across his features, softening the lines of grief that had once seemed etched into his skin.

"You know," Sean said suddenly, breaking the comfortable silence that had settled between them, "I haven't decorated a tree since...well, since before my wife passed away." His voice was soft, tinged with a hint of sadness that made Frankie's heart ache.

She reached out instinctively, laying a gentle hand on his arm. "I'm so sorry, Sean," she murmured, her voice thick with emotion. "I can't even imagine how difficult that must be."

He smiled sadly, covering her hand with his own. "It's been hard," he admitted, "but being here with you, doing this... it feels right. Like maybe it's time to start making new memories, you know?"

Frankie nodded, blinking back the tears that threatened to spill down her cheeks. "I think that's a beautiful way to look at it," she said softly, squeezing his hand. "And I'm honored to be a part of those new memories."

As the sun began to dip behind the horizon, casting the world in a soft, golden glow, Sean and Frankie stepped back to admire their handiwork. The tree glittered and shone, a beacon of hope and joy in the gathering dusk.

"It's perfect," Frankie breathed, leaning her head against Sean's shoulder. "Absolutely perfect."

Sean smiled down at her, his eyes soft with an emotion she couldn't quite name. "It really is," he agreed, wrapping an arm around her shoulders and pulling her close. "Thank you, Frankie. For everything."

As they stood there, watching the twinkling lights dance across the snow-covered ground, Sean felt a warmth blossom in his chest—a feeling he hadn't experienced in longer than he cared to remember. It was more than just the physical warmth of Frankie's body pressed against his own; it was the warmth of hope, of possibility, of a future that suddenly seemed brighter than it had in years.

He thought of Grace, of the way her eyes had sparkled with excitement when he'd told her about the festival, of the way her laughter had filled the house as she'd helped him pick out ornaments for the tree. And he thought of Frankie, of the way she'd waltzed into his life with her infectious smile and boundless enthusiasm, bringing with her a light that had slowly but surely begun to chase away the shadows of his grief.

Chapter Seven

Frankie smiled warmly at Sean as they hung the last string of twinkling lights on the community center's frosty window. His strong hands worked deftly, securing the delicate wires with care. As they stepped back to admire their handiwork, their shoulders brushed, sending a shiver down Frankie's spine that had nothing to do with the cold.

"It looks magical," Frankie breathed, her eyes bright with joy. "The children are going to love it."

Sean nodded, a soft smile playing at the corners of his lips. "You have a real gift for this, Frankie. Candy Cane Lane is lucky to have you."

A blush crept up Frankie's cheeks at the compliment. She found herself increasingly drawn to Sean's quiet strength and gentle spirit. But a flicker of doubt clouded her mind. Was he ready to open his heart again after losing his wife?

"I couldn't have done it without your help," she replied, nudging him playfully. "We make quite the team."

Just then, Grace bounded over, her cheeks rosy from the crisp winter air. "It's so pretty!"

Sean ruffled his daughter's hair affectionately. "Thanks, sweetheart. Frankie deserves most of the credit though."

Grace glanced between them, a mischievous twinkle in her eye. "Can Frankie come over for hot cocoa, Daddy?"

Frankie's heart skipped a beat at the suggestion. Sean looked momentarily taken aback, but then a warm smile spread across his face. "That's a wonderful idea, Grace. Frankie, would you like to join us for cocoa and cookies this weekend?"

Frankie beamed, her faith in the magic of the season growing stronger by the minute. "I'd love to, Sean. Thank you."

As they parted ways, Frankie couldn't help but feel that God was working in mysterious and wonderful ways, weaving together the threads of their lives into a beautiful tapestry. She couldn't wait to see what the future held.

Frankie stepped into the warmth of the church, the scent of candles and pine enveloping her. She smiled as her new friend, Sarah, waved her over to a pew.

"Frankie, you look like you have a lot on your mind," Sarah said, her kind eyes filled with concern. "Is everything okay?"

Sighing, Frankie sat down beside her. "It's just...I think I'm falling for Sean, but I don't know if he's ready for a new relationship after losing his wife."

Sarah placed a comforting hand on Frankie's shoulder. "I understand your hesitation, but have faith. God works in mysterious ways, and if it's meant to be, He'll guide you both."

Frankie nodded, finding solace in Sarah's words. "You're right. I need to trust in His plan and let things unfold naturally."

As they bowed their heads in prayer, Frankie felt a sense of peace wash over her, knowing that no matter what challenges lay ahead, her faith would see her through.

The next day, Frankie bustled around the festival

site, her mind preoccupied with the impending decoration crisis. The snowstorm had delayed the shipment, and she was running out of time.

"Please, Lord," she whispered, her breath forming tiny clouds in the frigid air. "I need your guidance now more than ever."

Just then, her phone buzzed with an incoming call. It was the supplier, apologizing profusely for the delay and promising to do everything in their power to get the decorations to her as soon as possible.

Frankie thanked them, trying to quell the rising panic in her chest. She surveyed the half-decorated space, her mind racing with contingency plans.

"I can do this," she murmured, squaring her shoulders. "I just need to have faith and think creatively."

With renewed determination, Frankie set about making do with what she had, repurposing old decorations and enlisting the help of volunteers to craft handmade ornaments. As she worked, she felt her anxiety begin to dissipate, replaced by a growing sense of hope and purpose.

As Frankie rummaged through a box of old decorations, she heard a familiar voice behind her. "Need a hand?" Sean asked, his warm smile instantly putting her at ease.

Frankie turned, her eyes widening in surprise. "Sean! I didn't expect to see you here. I thought you'd be busy with your own holiday preparations."

He shrugged, his gaze sweeping over the half-decorated space. "Sarah mentioned you might need some help, and I couldn't let you tackle this alone. Besides, I've been known to get creative with wood and paint from time to time."

Frankie's heart swelled with gratitude. "That would be amazing, Sean. Thank you." She handed him a box of wooden ornaments, and they set to work, their conversation flowing easily as they painted and adorned the pieces.

As they worked side by side, Frankie couldn't help but marvel at Sean's skill and attention to detail. He transformed the simple wooden shapes into intricate, beautiful decorations, each one bearing his unique artistic touch.

"These are incredible," Frankie breathed, holding up a delicately painted snowflake. "You have a real gift."

He ducked his head, a shy smile playing on his lips. "Thanks, Frankie. It's been a while since I've had the chance to create something just for the joy of it."

As the hours passed, the festival site began to take shape, transformed by their combined efforts. The handmade decorations lent a warm, inviting atmosphere, and Frankie could feel the love and care that had gone into each piece.

"I can't believe we did it," she said, her voice filled with wonder. "When I thought all was lost, you stepped in and made it even better than I could have imagined."

Sean placed a gentle hand on her shoulder, his eyes shining with understanding. "Sometimes, it takes a challenge to show us what we're truly capable of, and to remind us that we're never alone."

Frankie nodded, her heart full. She looked around at the transformed space, at the people working together in harmony, and felt a profound sense of God's presence. Through the trials and the triumphs, He had been there, guiding her steps and bringing people into her life to support and uplift her.

As the festival drew near, Frankie knew that whatever challenges lay ahead, her faith would see her through. And with Sean by her side, she felt a newfound strength and resilience, ready to face whatever the future might bring.

***

Sean stood back, admiring the festive scene

before him. The twinkling lights, the handcrafted decorations, and the joyful laughter of the volunteers filled the air with a warmth that seeped into his heart. His gaze drifted to Frankie, who was directing the placement of a garland with her signature enthusiasm.

"A little to the left...perfect!" she exclaimed, her face glowing with satisfaction.

As he watched her, Sean felt a stirring in his chest, a flicker of something he hadn't experienced in a long time. The way Frankie's eyes sparkled when she smiled, the gentle touch of her hand on his arm as she thanked him for his help—it all awakened a part of him he thought had been lost forever.

"What do you think?" Frankie asked, turning to him with an expectant look.

He blinked, realizing he'd been staring. "It's...it's beautiful, Frankie. You've done an incredible job bringing everyone together to make this happen."

She beamed at him, and his heart skipped a beat. "I couldn't have done it without you, Sean. Your decorations are the heart of this festival."

As the day wore on and the preparations neared completion, Sean found himself gravitating towards Frankie, seeking her company and basking in her presence. They worked side by side, talking and laughing, their hands brushing occasionally as they reached for the same ornament or strand of lights.

But even as he reveled in the joy of their connection, a flicker of doubt crept into Sean's mind. Was he ready to open his heart again? Could he risk the pain of loss, the fear of letting someone in only to have them taken away?

He glanced at the wedding band he still wore, a symbol of the love he had shared with his late wife. The memories of their life together, the laughter and the tears, the plans they had made—they all seemed to blur together in a bittersweet haze.

Frankie's voice broke through his thoughts. "Sean, are you alright?"

He looked up to find her standing before him, her brow furrowed with concern. In that moment, he realized that the warmth and compassion in her eyes held the promise of something new, something beautiful that could grow from the ashes of his grief.

"I'm okay," he said softly, offering her a small smile. "Just lost in thought for a moment."

Frankie reached out, giving his hand a gentle squeeze. "If you ever need to talk, I'm here."

Sean nodded, his heart swelling with gratitude.

As they turned back to their tasks, he knew that the path ahead would not be easy. But with Frankie by his side and faith in his heart, he felt a glimmer of hope that perhaps, just perhaps, he could learn to love again.

Chapter Eight

Frankie stepped back and admired the twinkling lights draped along Candy Cane Lane, their warm glow casting a magical aura over the festival grounds. The scent of cinnamon and pine mingled in the crisp winter air, filling her with a sense of nostalgia and joy.

"Well, if it isn't our very own Christmas angel!" a familiar voice called out. Frankie spun around to see her parents, arms laden with boxes of decorations, their faces beaming with pride.

"Mom! Dad!" Frankie rushed over and embraced them tightly. "I wasn't expecting you until later. What a wonderful surprise!"

Her mother, Evelyn, cupped Frankie's face in her hands. "We couldn't wait to see all the magic you've been creating here, sweetie. It looks absolutely enchanting."

Frank, Frankie's father, nodded in agreement. "Your mother's right, pumpkin. This festival is going to be the talk of the town. You've really outdone yourself."

Frankie felt her cheeks flush with a mix of pride and gratitude. "Thanks, Mom and Dad. I couldn't have done it without the help of so many amazing people, like Sean and his daughter Grace."

Evelyn and Frank exchanged a knowing glance. "Speaking of Sean," Evelyn began gently, "how are things going between you two?"

Frankie's heart skipped a beat and her cheeks colored. Of course, she'd confided in her mom about her growing feelings for Sean. Her mother had always been her best friend and she told her everything.

She couldn't deny the growing connection she felt with Sean, but doubt crept in. "Oh, we're just friends, Mom. He's been through so much, and I don't want to complicate things."

Her parents shared a knowing look before Frank placed a comforting hand on his daughter's shoulder. "Frankie, love has a way of finding us when we least expect it. Trust in God's plan and open your heart to the possibilities."

Evelyn nodded, her eyes shining with wisdom. "Your father's right, dear. Have faith that everything will unfold as it should. Just remember to be true to yourself and let your light shine."

Frankie hugged her parents tightly, their words of encouragement filling her with renewed hope and determination. "Thanks, Mom and Dad. I love you both so much."

As her parents headed off to assist with the decorations, Frankie turned her attention back to Candy Cane Lane. She reached for the mistletoe, ready to hang it as the finishing touch, when a warm hand brushed against hers. Startled, she looked up to find Sean's gentle eyes gazing down at her.

"Sorry, I didn't mean to startle you," Sean apologized, a sheepish grin on his face. "I just wanted to see if you needed any help."

Frankie's heart fluttered as they stood there, fingers intertwined around the delicate sprig. "No worries, I'm glad you're here," she replied softly.

Together, they hung the mistletoe, its presence a symbol of the love and hope that filled the air.

Frankie and Sean stepped back, admiring the

mistletoe as it hung delicately amidst the twinkling lights of Candy Cane Lane. The festival grounds were transformed, a veritable winter wonderland that seemed to sparkle with the promise of magic and romance.

As they stood there, shoulders brushing, Frankie couldn't help but steal a glance at Sean. The soft glow of the Christmas lights danced across his handsome features, illuminating the gentle smile that played on his lips. His eyes, usually tinged with a hint of sadness, now shimmered with warmth and affection.

Sean turned to face Frankie, his gaze locking with hers. In that moment, the world around them seemed to fade away, leaving only the two of them wrapped in the enchantment of the season. He reached out, gently tucking a stray curl behind her ear, his fingers lingering on her cheek.

"Frankie," he whispered, his voice low and tender, "I can't thank you enough for everything you've done. Not just for the festival, but for Grace and me. You've brought so much light into our lives."

Frankie's heart swelled with emotion, her eyes glistening with unshed tears of joy. "Sean, you and Grace have been such a blessing to me. I never knew I could feel this way, but being with you both feels like coming home."

As they spoke, snowflakes began to drift down from the sky, dusting their hair and shoulders with a glittering layer of white. The air was crisp and clean, filled with the scent of hot cocoa and freshly baked gingerbread. Soft strains of Christmas carols floated on the breeze, adding to the dreamlike atmosphere.

Sean's hand found Frankie's, their fingers inter-twining as if they were always meant to be joined. He drew her closer, until they were standing toe-to-toe, their breaths mingling in the frosty air. Frankie's pulse raced, her skin tingling with anticipation and longing.

Frankie's free hand came up to rest on Sean's chest, feeling the steady beat of his heart beneath her palm.

Their faces inched closer, drawn by an irresistible force. As their lips met beneath the mistletoe, the world around them erupted in a symphony of sensations.

The softness of the snowflakes, the warmth of their embrace, the sweetness of their kiss - it all blended together in a perfect moment of bliss. Frankie melted into Sean's arms, losing herself in the tender caress of his lips on hers. It was as if all the love and longing they had been holding back was poured into that one enchanted kiss.

When they finally parted, breathless and flushed, Sean rested his forehead against Frankie's.

Neither of them spoke, both afraid to ruin the perfect moment, but something silently shifted between them, and

unbeknownst to them, a small figure peeked out from behind a nearby Christmas tree, her eyes wide with delight. Grace grinned from ear to ear, her heart bursting with happiness as she watched her father and Frankie together. She wanted more than anything for Frankie to be her new mom, and she knew just how to make it happen.

Chapter Nine

Across town, Frankie stood amidst the bustling activity of the festival setup. Twinkling lights sparkled overhead, casting a warm glow on the joyful faces of the volunteers. The scent of pine and cinnamon filled the air, mingling with the laughter and chatter of the townsfolk.

As Frankie surveyed the scene, pride swelled in her chest. The event was coming together beautifully, each element a testament to the community's love and dedication. Yet, a nagging worry tugged at the corner of her mind. Would it be enough? Would the festival draw the crowds they so desperately needed?

She'd put all her advertising resources to use,

trying her best to get the turn-out the little town so desperately needed.

"Frankie, you've truly outdone yourself!" Mrs. Jameson exclaimed, her eyes wide with wonder as she took in the transformed town square. "I've never seen anything so magical!"

Frankie beamed at the compliment, her heart warming at the sight of the elderly woman's happiness. "Thank you, Mrs. Jameson. It means the world to me to see everyone coming together like this."

As more townspeople arrived, their excited whispers and gasps of delight filled the air. Children raced through the streets, their laughter ringing out like bells. Couples strolled hand in hand, eyes sparkling with the promise of romance.

Frankie watched it all, her heart swelling with a mix of joy and apprehension. She knew the festival had the power to bring hope and healing to the town, but the weight of responsibility rested heavily on her shoulders. She closed her eyes for a moment, sending up a silent prayer. "Please, God, let this be enough. Let the festival be a success, and bring happiness to all who attend."

As if in answer to her prayer, a gentle hand touched her shoulder. Frankie turned to find Sean standing beside her, his eyes soft with understanding.

"It's amazing, Frankie. You've worked so hard, and it shows. Have faith."

Frankie leaned into his touch, drawing strength from his presence. "Thank you, Sean. I couldn't have done it without you." Together, they stood, watching as the town came alive with the magic of the holiday season, each lost in their own thoughts of love, family, and the power of believing.

Sean returned home that evening, his mind still buzzing with the day's events. The festival was a huge success, and it was all thanks to Frankie.

He was still smiling as he hung his coat by the door and went through the mail. His heart warmed when he saw the letter addressed to Santa in Grace's childish scrawl.

With a smile, Sean settled into his favorite armchair and began to read. As his eyes scanned the words, his smile slowly faded, replaced by a look of tender understanding.

> *Dear Santa,*
> *I know I usually ask for toys and games, but this year, I have a different*

wish. My daddy has been so sad since Mommy went to heaven. I want him to be happy again. Please, Santa, can you help him find love and laughter? I think Miss Frankie makes him smile. Plus, I really like her and think she would make a great mommy for me. Thank you, Santa.
Love,
Grace

Sean felt a lump form in his throat as he reread the letter, his vision blurring with unshed tears. He had been so focused on his own grief that he hadn't realized how much Grace had been affected, how much she wanted him to find happiness again.

His thoughts drifted to Frankie, the way her smile lit up a room, the way she made him feel alive again. But doubt crept in, the fear of opening his heart, of risking the pain of loss once more.

The next morning, Sean found himself sitting in the small church office, seeking the guidance of Pastor Matthews. The older man listened intently as Sean poured out his heart, speaking of his growing feelings for Frankie and the fear that held him back.

"Sean," Pastor Matthews began, his voice gentle but firm, "I understand your hesitation. Losing a loved one is a pain like no other, and the thought of loving again can be terrifying. But God's love is infinite, and He wants us to experience the joy and healing that comes from opening our hearts."

He leaned forward, catching Sean's gaze. "Love is a risk, but it's a risk worth taking. It's not about replacing what you've lost, but about making room for new blessings. Trust in God's plan, and let Him guide you on this journey."

Sean nodded, his heart feeling lighter than it had in years. "Thank you, Pastor. I think I needed to hear that."

As he left the church, Sean felt a newfound sense of hope and determination. He knew that loving again would take courage, but with God's help and Grace's blessing, he was ready to take that leap of faith.

The twinkling lights of Candy Cane Lane cast a warm glow across Frankie's face as she sat on a bench, her eyes sparkling with the reflection of the festive display. Sean approached quietly, his heart racing as he took a seat beside her. The air between them was charged with a mix of anticipation and uncertainty.

"It's beautiful, isn't it?" Frankie whispered, her gaze fixed on the shimmering lights. "The way the colors dance and the world seems to slow down, just for a moment."

Sean nodded, his eyes never leaving her face. "It is. But not as beautiful as the woman who made it all happen."

Frankie turned to him, a soft blush coloring her cheeks. "Sean, I..." She paused, searching for the right words. "I don't know what to say."

Sean reached for her hand, his fingers intertwining with hers. "Frankie, you've brought light back into my life. You've shown me that it's possible to find joy and laughter again, even after the darkest of times. And I've been scared to admit it, but I'm falling for you."

Frankie's heart soared at his words, but she could see the hesitation in his eyes. "I care about you deeply, and I want nothing more than to explore these feelings. But I also understand if you're not ready. I know that loving again takes time and courage."

Sean took a deep breath, his thumb gently caressing the back of her hand. "I am scared, Frankie. Scared of opening my heart again, of risking the pain of loss. But I'm also scared of letting this chance slip away. I've been talking to Pastor Matthews, and he reminded me that love is a risk worth taking."

Frankie smiled, her eyes shining with unshed tears. "Love is always a leap of faith. But I believe that God has brought us together for a reason, and I'm willing to take that leap with you if you are."

Sean pulled her closer, his forehead resting against hers. "I can't promise that it will be easy, but I can promise that I'll try. I want to see where this path leads us, Frankie. Together."

As they sat there, wrapped in each other's embrace, the Christmas lights seemed to dance with renewed vigor, as if celebrating the love and hope that had blossomed beneath their glow. Sean pressed his lips to Frankie's for the second time, this time with the understanding that there was indeed something between them.

Chapter Ten

The winter sun cast a warm glow across Sean's workshop as he carefully sanded a wooden rocking horse, the sawdust dancing in the afternoon light. Frankie leaned against the doorframe, admiring his craftsmanship and the gentle expression on his face. A smile played at her lips as she stepped inside.

"Knock, knock," she said softly, not wanting to startle him.

Sean looked up, his eyes crinkling at the corners as a grin spread across his face. "Well, hello there. To what do I owe the pleasure of your company on this fine day?"

Frankie crossed the room, her boots crunching on wood shavings, and perched on the edge of his workbench. "Can't a girl just drop by to see her favorite carpenter?" She winked playfully.

He set down the sandpaper and turned to face her fully, wiping his hands on a rag. "Of course. I'm always happy to see you, Frankie." His voice was warm and sincere, making her heart flutter.

They had been officially dating for a week now, but were taking things slow, letting their relationship grow naturally rooted in their shared faith. Frankie knew Sean was still healing from losing his wife, and she wanted to give him the space and time he needed.

She fidgeted with the zipper of her coat, suddenly nervous. "Actually, I did want to talk to you about something..."

Sean's brow furrowed slightly with concern. "Is everything alright?" He reached out and took her hand, his thumb rubbing soothing circles on her skin.

"Yes, everything's fine. It's just..." She took a deep breath. "I got a job offer. To plan a big event in Pinewood Falls."

"Frankie, that's wonderful!" Sean's face lit up with genuine happiness for her. "You're so talented, you deserve this opportunity."

She smiled at his enthusiasm, but it didn't quite reach her eyes. "Thanks. It is exciting. But Pinewood

Falls is an hour away. I'd have to be there a lot over the next month leading up to the event..."

Understanding dawned in Sean's expression. "Meaning a lot of time away from Candy Cane Lane. Away from Grace and me."

Frankie nodded, glancing down at their intertwined hands. She didn't want to pressure him, but her heart whispered that what they had was special, worth fighting for. Worth staying for.

"I haven't accepted yet. I wanted to talk to you first, see how you felt about it." She looked up at him through her lashes. "This...us...it's important to me. I don't want to mess it up by being gone all the time right when we're starting out."

Sean was quiet for a moment, his gaze distant as if deep in thought. Then he squeezed her hand and met her eyes, a soft smile on his lips.

"Frankie, I appreciate you considering my feelings. But I don't ever want to hold you back from chasing your dreams." His other hand came up to cradle her cheek. "Let's pray about it together, and trust that God will guide us on the right path, wherever that leads. All I know is, whether near or far, I'm in this with you."

Tears pricked at the corners of Frankie's eyes, moved by his understanding and steadfast support.

Unable to find the right words, she simply leaned forward and captured his lips in a sweet, lingering kiss, pouring all her gratitude and affection into the gesture.

When they parted, foreheads resting together, Frankie knew that no matter what she decided, they would weather it together, sustained by unshakable faith, finding strength in each other and the love growing between them—beautiful and resilient, like the wood taking shape beneath Sean's hands, with God as their guide.

Sean grabbed Frankie's hand and led her into his workshop, a secretive smile playing at the corners of his mouth. The scent of fresh wood shavings and varnish enveloped them as they stepped inside the cozy space, lit by the warm glow of string lights draped along the rafters.

"I have something special for you," Sean said softly, guiding her towards his workbench where a small, cloth-covered object rested. With a gentle tug, he revealed a beautifully crafted wooden ornament, intricately carved with swirling patterns that seemed to dance in the soft light.

Frankie gasped, her fingers hovering over the smooth surface, almost afraid to touch the delicate masterpiece. "Sean, it's stunning," she whispered, eyes wide with wonder. "Did you make this?"

He nodded, a shy grin spreading across his face. "I wanted to create something that would always remind us of our first Christmas together. See this intertwining design? It represents our paths converging, our lives becoming one."

Tears glistened in Frankie's eyes as she traced the flowing lines, her heart swelling with love and gratitude. "I'll treasure it forever," she murmured, rising on her tiptoes to press a tender kiss to his cheek.

Just then, the patter of small feet announced Grace's arrival. "Daddy! Frankie!" she exclaimed, bounding into the workshop with a vibrant drawing clutched in her hand. "Look what I made for our Christmas tree!"

The couple crouched down to admire the colorful picture, stick figures representing their little family, surrounded by hearts and stars. Grace pointed to each character, her voice brimming with excitement. "That's you, Daddy, and that's Frankie, and there's me in the middle!"

Sean laughed, ruffling his daughter's hair affectionately. "It's perfect, Gracie. We'll hang it right next to Frankie's ornament."

Frankie felt a lump form in her throat as she

gazed at the two people who had become her world. "I love it, sweetie," she said, pulling Grace into a warm hug.

Grace's small arms tightened around Frankie's neck, her innocent words filled with certainty. "You're what I asked Santa for."

In that moment, surrounded by the love and acceptance radiating from Sean and Grace, Frankie felt a sense of peace wash over her. This was where she was meant to be—in the embrace of a family forged by faith, bound by love, and blessed with the promise of a future filled with joy and togetherness.

As they hung the ornaments side by side on the workshop's tiny tree, Frankie's heart soared with the knowledge that she had finally found her true home, not in a place, but in the hearts of the two people who loved her unconditionally, guided by the grace of God.

The warm glow of candlelight bathed the church in a soft, reverent ambiance as Frankie, Sean, and Grace settled into their pew on Christmas Eve. The scent of pine and incense mingled in the air, creating an atmosphere of peaceful solemnity.

Frankie's hand found Sean's, their fingers intertwining as they shared a smile that spoke volumes about the love and gratitude they felt in that moment.

As the choir's voices rose in harmony, singing traditional carols that echoed through the sanctuary, Frankie felt a profound sense of belonging. She glanced at Grace, who sat between them, her eyes wide with wonder as she absorbed the beauty of the service. Sean's arm draped protectively around his daughter's shoulders, a gesture that now extended to include Frankie, making her feel cherished and secure.

The pastor's words washed over them, speaking of hope, love, and the miraculous gift of a savior born in a humble manger. Frankie's heart swelled with emotion as she reflected on the blessings that had brought her to this moment—the job in Candy Cane Lane, the chance encounter with Sean and Grace, and the way their lives had become beautifully entwined.

As the congregation bowed their heads in prayer, Frankie closed her eyes, her soul overflowing with gratitude as she prayed silently. *Dear God, thank you for leading me here, for bringing Sean and Grace into my life. Thank you for opening my heart to love again, for showing me that your plan is greater than anything I could have imagined.*

Tears of joy slipped down her cheeks as she continued, *I am so grateful for this family, for the love and acceptance they have given me. Please guide us as we continue on this journey together, and help me to be the best partner and mother I can be. Amen.*

As the final notes of "Silent Night" filled the church, Frankie felt Sean's hand squeeze hers, a silent affirmation of the love and commitment they shared. Grace leaned her head against Frankie's shoulder, her small hand reaching up to touch the locket that hung around Frankie's neck—another gift from Sean that held a picture of the three of them, a symbol of their unbreakable bond.

In that sacred moment, surrounded by the warmth of family and the presence of God, Frankie knew that she had found her true purpose. Candy Cane Lane had given her more than just a fresh start; it had given her a home, a family, and a love that would last a lifetime.

Epilogue

FOUR YEARS LATER

The aroma of freshly brewed coffee and sizzling bacon filled the cozy kitchen as Frankie moved about, her hips swaying to the rhythm of "Jingle Bells." She flipped a pancake with a flick of her wrist, smiling as it landed perfectly in the center of the skillet. Though her movements were slightly slower these days, her growing baby bump a constant reminder of the precious life within, Frankie couldn't contain the joy that radiated from her very core.

"Someone's in the Christmas spirit," a warm voice chuckled from behind her. Strong arms encircled her waist as Sean pulled her close, his hands coming to rest gently on her rounded belly. Frankie leaned back into his embrace, relishing the comfort and love that enveloped her.

"How can I not be? It's Christmas, and we're fixing to be a family of four," she beamed, turning her head to meet his affectionate gaze.

Sean chuckled, his breath tickling her ear. "I can't wait to meet our little miracle. Grace is going to be the best big sister."

Frankie's heart swelled at the thought of their daughter, so eager and loving. She placed her hands over Sean's, their fingers intertwining as they cradled their unborn child. "We're so blessed, Sean. I never imagined I could be this happy."

"Me neither," he whispered, pressing a tender kiss to her temple. "You've brought so much light into our lives, Frankie. I thank God every day for you."

Frankie turned in his arms, her green eyes sparkling with unshed tears of joy. "I love you, Sean Morrison. You and Grace mean everything to me."

As they stood there, lost in each other's embrace, the scent of burning pancakes jolted Frankie back to reality. She laughed, quickly turning off the stove and moving the skillet to a cool burner. "Oops! Guess I got a little distracted."

Sean grinned, swiping a piece of bacon from the

plate. "Distracted by my irresistible charm, no doubt."

Frankie swatted at him playfully, her laughter ringing through the kitchen. "More like your irresistible appetite! Now, let's get this breakfast on the table before our little elf wakes up. We've got a big day ahead of us."

Grace bounded into the kitchen, her blonde curls bouncing with each step. "Mommy, Daddy, guess what?" she exclaimed, her eyes sparkling with excitement. "I have the best idea for decorating the baby's nursery!"

Frankie smiled warmly, setting a plate of pancakes on the table. "Oh, really? Tell us all about it, sweetheart."

"Well," Grace began, gesturing animatedly, "I think we should paint the walls like a magical forest, with tall trees and twinkling stars. And we can hang a mobile with little woodland animals over the crib!"

Sean chuckled, ruffling his daughter's hair affectionately. "That sounds enchanting, Gracie. I think your little brother or sister will love it."

Grace beamed, her face radiating pure joy. "And I

can read bedtime stories to the baby, just like you and Mommy read to me. I'll be the best big sister ever!"

Frankie felt her heart swell with love and pride. Grace might not be hers biologically, but she was her daughter in every other way that counted. She loved her just like she was her own, and it always warmed her heart when she called her 'mommy' so readily. *Our little girl is growing up so fast*, she thought, blinking back happy tears. *She's going to be such a wonderful role model for our new addition.*

As the family finished their breakfast, Sean glanced out the window, taking in the gentle snowfall. "Who's ready for a special Christmas adventure?" he asked, his eyes twinkling with anticipation.

"Me, me!" Grace squealed, bouncing in her seat. "Where are we going, Daddy?"

"We're heading to Candy Cane Lane to pick out an ornament for the baby's first Christmas," Sean revealed, watching his daughter's face light up with delight.

Frankie smiled, her heart full of gratitude for these precious moments. "Let's bundle up, then. We don't want to keep the magic waiting."

The family donned their coats, hats, and gloves, stepping out into the crisp winter air. The snow crunched beneath their feet as they walked hand in hand, their laughter echoing through the quiet streets. Grace skipped ahead, her red scarf trailing behind her like a festive banner.

This is what the holidays are all about, Frankie mused, leaning into Sean's warmth. *Family, love, and the promise of new beginnings.* She placed a gentle hand on her growing belly, silently thanking God for the miracles in her life.

As they approached Candy Cane Lane, the twinkling lights and vibrant decorations came into view, casting a warm glow over the snowy landscape. Grace's eyes widened with wonder, her excitement palpable in the frosty air.

"Look at all the pretty lights!" she gasped, pointing at the glittering storefronts. "Can we go in every shop, Mommy? Please?"

Frankie laughed, squeezing her daughter's hand. "We'll see, sweetheart. Let's start with the ornament store and go from there."

The quaint ornament shop beckoned with its display of colorful baubles and shimmering tinsel. As they stepped inside, a cheerful bell chimed above the door, announcing their arrival. The warm scent of cinnamon and pine enveloped them, instantly transporting them into a winter wonderland.

Grace darted towards the shelves, her eyes

dancing with delight as she took in the array of ornaments. From glittering snowflakes to whimsical woodland creatures, each piece seemed to hold a special charm. Sean and Frankie followed close behind, their hands intertwined, sharing amused glances at their daughter's unbridled enthusiasm.

"Remember, Gracie," Sean reminded gently, "we're here to find a special ornament for the baby's first Christmas."

Grace nodded solemnly, her brow furrowing with determination. She surveyed the shelves, carefully examining each ornament with the seriousness of a curator. Her small hands reached out, hovering over a shimmering reindeer, then a jolly snowman, before finally settling on a delicate angel.

The porcelain figure had a serene expression, with gossamer wings and a flowing gown that seemed to capture the very essence of grace. Grace cradled the ornament in her hands, a soft smile playing on her lips.

"This one," she declared, holding it up for her parents to see. "The angel will watch over the baby, just like I will. I'm going to be the best big sister ever!"

Frankie's heart swelled with love and pride as she knelt beside her daughter. "It's perfect, sweetheart. The baby is so lucky to have you as a big sister."

Sean placed a gentle hand on Grace's shoulder, his eyes shining with emotion. "You're going to be amazing, Gracie. The baby will always have an angel looking out for them, both on the tree and in their life."

As they made their way to the counter, the ornament carefully nestled in Grace's hands, Frankie couldn't help but feel a sense of awe at the love and unity that surrounded them. In this moment, amidst the twinkling lights and festive cheer, she knew that their family was truly blessed.

The shopkeeper, a kindly old man with a twinkle in his eye, carefully took the angel ornament from Grace's hands. "Ah, what a lovely choice, young lady," he said, his voice warm and gentle. "This angel will bring lots of love and protection to your new little one."

Grace beamed with pride as the shopkeeper wrapped the ornament in tissue paper, nestling it gently in a festive box. He tied a shimmering ribbon around it, creating a perfect bow. Sean and Frankie exchanged a knowing smile, their hearts full of gratitude for their thoughtful daughter.

As they stepped out of the shop, the crisp winter

air greeted them, carrying with it the faint scent of cinnamon and pine. The walk home was filled with laughter and excited chatter, Grace skipping ahead, the precious box held close to her heart.

Back at home, the family gathered in the living room, the Christmas tree standing tall and proud in the corner. The twinkling lights cast a warm glow across the room, and the scent of fresh pine mingled with the aroma of hot cocoa wafting in from the kitchen.

Sean carefully lifted Grace, allowing her to place the angel ornament on a prominent branch. As she stepped back, the angel seemed to shimmer, its porcelain features catching the light. Frankie felt a lump form in her throat, overcome with emotion at the sight of their growing family represented on the tree.

"It's beautiful," she whispered, leaning into Sean's embrace. "Our little angel, watching over us all."

Sean pressed a gentle kiss to her temple, his strong arms holding her close. "Just like you, my love. You're the heart of this family, the one who brings us all together."

Sean and Frankie stood there for a moment, foreheads touching, basking in the glow of their shared love and gratitude. The soft strains of Christmas carols played in the background, mingling with the sound of Grace's happy humming as she continued to decorate the tree.

In that moment, surrounded by the warmth and love of their family, Sean and Frankie knew that they were truly blessed. Whatever the future might hold, they would face it together, secure in the knowledge that their faith and love would guide them through.

Excerpt from Ruth

Light filtered through the lace curtains, casting intricate shadows across the faded wallpaper. Ruth sat in the old wooden chair by the window, her hands folded in her lap. She gazed out at the quiet street, the stillness broken only by the occasional rustling of leaves in the gentle breeze. In the silence, memories flooded her mind, carrying her back to the life she had shared with her beloved husband.

She recalled their first meeting, a chance encounter at a bustling coffee shop. His warm smile and kind eyes had drawn her in, sparking a connection that would grow into something beautiful and profound. They had built a life together, navigating the joys and challenges that came their way. Through laughter and tears, triumphs and setbacks, their love had been the constant that anchored them.

But now, in the aftermath of his passing, Ruth found herself adrift, struggling to find her footing in this new reality. The weight of grief pressed heavily upon her heart, a constant companion that shadowed her every step. She yearned for his comforting presence, his gentle touch, and the sound of his voice that had always soothed her troubled soul.

With a sigh, Ruth stood and made her way to the kitchen, her footsteps echoing in the empty house. She opened the cabinet, reaching for a mug, but paused as her fingers brushed against the chipped one he had always favored. A bittersweet smile tugged at her lips as she remembered the countless mornings they had shared, sipping coffee and planning their day.

As she prepared her tea, Ruth's thoughts turned to the pressing matters at hand. The move to this small town had been a necessary step, a chance for her and Naomi to find solace and support in the close-knit community. Yet, the financial challenges loomed large, casting a shadow over their already fragile existence.

Ruth had spent countless hours scouring job listings, her hope dwindling with each rejection. The skills she had honed in the city seemed of little use here, where opportunities were scarce and competition fierce. She worried for Naomi, who had already endured so much loss, and the burden of providing for them both weighed heavily on her shoulders.

"Lord, please guide me," she whispered, her eyes closing as she leaned against the counter. "Show me the way forward, and grant me the strength to face whatever lies ahead."

As the steam from her tea curled upward, Ruth felt a flicker of determination ignite within her. She had weathered storms before, and with faith and perseverance, she would find a way through this one as well. For Naomi's sake, and for the memory of the love she had shared with her husband, Ruth would not give up.

With renewed resolve, she returned to the window, her gaze fixed on the horizon. The path ahead was uncertain, but Ruth knew that she would face it with the same quiet strength and resilience that had carried her this far. In this new chapter of her life, she would find purpose and hope, guided by the unwavering love that still lived within her heart.

The gentle creak of the floorboards announced Naomi's presence, and Ruth turned to see her mother-in-law's weathered face etched with concern. Naomi's eyes, once bright with joy, now held a shadow of the grief that had become their constant companion. She approached Ruth slowly, her steps measured and heavy, as if the weight of their shared sorrow had settled into her very bones.

"Oh, my dear girl," Naomi murmured, her voice a soothing balm against the silence. She reached out, her work-worn hands clasping Ruth's own, and in that simple gesture, a flicker of warmth passed between them. "I know the road ahead seems daunting, but you mustn't lose heart."

Ruth's throat tightened, emotion threatening to overtake her. She looked down at their intertwined fingers, drawing strength from the connection. "I just...I don't know how to make it right, Naomi. I've tried so hard to find work, to provide for us, but it feels like every door is closed."

Naomi's gaze softened, a sad smile tugging at the corners of her mouth. "You've already done so much, Ruth. More than I could ever have asked." She gently cupped Ruth's cheek, tilting her face upward until their eyes met. "Your love, your loyalty...it's a balm to my weary soul. You are a blessing, and together, we will find our way."

Tears spilled down Ruth's cheeks, and she leaned into Naomi's touch, allowing herself a moment of vulnerability. The weight of their shared grief hung heavy in the air, a palpable presence that seemed to seep into the very walls of their modest home.

"I miss him," Ruth whispered, her voice barely audible. "I miss the life we had, the dreams we shared. And sometimes...sometimes I fear I'll never find that kind of love again."

Naomi drew Ruth into a tight embrace, her own tears mingling with her daughter-in-law's. "Oh, my sweet girl," she murmured, her words muffled against Ruth's hair. "The love you and my son shared...it was a rare and beautiful thing. But I know, with all my heart, that you will find happiness again. You have so much light within you, so much to give."

As they clung to each other, the warmth of Naomi's love enveloped Ruth, a soothing balm against the ache of loss. In that moment, Ruth knew that though their path was marked by sorrow, they would face it together, drawing strength from the unbreakable bond they shared.

And somewhere, deep within her heart, a flicker

of hope began to grow, a tiny spark amidst the darkness. For even in the midst of their grief, Ruth knew that the love they had lost would forever be a part of them, guiding them forward into a future where healing and new beginnings awaited.

Keep reading Ruth here: Ruth

About the Author

Award-winning author Kayla Lowe writes women's fiction that explores complex themes with sensitivity and depth. Kayla's books delve into the intricacies of relationships, self-discovery, and resilience. From cozy love stories interspersed with a bit of faith to heartwarming tales of friendship and suspenseful novels of empowerment and heartbreak, her books illustrate the struggles specific to women.

When she's not churning out her next novel, you can find her with her feet in the sand and a book in her hand or curled up on the couch with her dogs.

Visit her website at www.authorkaylalowe.com.

Also by Kayla Lowe

<u>Series</u>

<u>Women of the Bible Fiction</u>

<u>Ruth</u>

<u>Esther</u>

<u>Rachel</u>

<u>Hannah</u>

<u>Deborah</u>

<u>Charms of the Chaste Court</u>

A Courtship in Covent Garden

Whispers in Westminster

Romance in Regent's Park

Serenade on Strand Street

Treasure in Tower Bridge

Sweet Honey by the Sea

The Beekeeper's Secret (Book 1)

A Royal Honeycomb (Book 2)

Bees in Blossom (Book 3)

Honeyed Kisses (Book 4)

Blooming Forever (Book 5)

Strawberry Beach Series

Beachside Lessons (Book 1)

Beachside Lessons (Book 2)

Beachside Lessons (Book 3)

Panama City Beach Series

Sun-Kissed Secrets (Book 1)

Sun-Kissed Secrets (Book 2)

Sun-Kissed Secrets (Book 3)

The Tainted Love Saga

Of Love and Deception (Book 1)

Of Love and Family (Book 2)

Of Love and Violence (Book 3)

Of Love and Abuse(Book 4)

Of Love and Crime (Book 5)

Of Love and Addiction (Book 6)

Of Love and Redemption (Book 7)

<u>Standalones</u>

Maiden's Blush

<u>Poetry</u>

Phantom Poetry

Lost and Found